Dear Parent:

Congratulations! Your child is taking the first steps on an exciting journey. The destination? Independent reading!

STEP INTO READING® will help your child get there. The program offers five steps to reading success. Each step includes fun stories and colorful art. There are also Step into Reading Sticker Books, Step into Reading Math Readers, Step into Reading Phonics Readers, Step into Reading Write-In Readers, and Step into Reading Phonics Boxed Sets—a complete literacy program with something for every child.

Learning to Read, Step by Step!

Ready to Read   Preschool–Kindergarten
• big type and easy words • rhyme and rhythm • picture clues
For children who know the alphabet and are eager to begin reading.

Reading with Help   Preschool–Grade 1
• basic vocabulary • short sentences • simple stories
For children who recognize familiar words and sound out new words with help.

Reading on Your Own   Grades 1–3
• engaging characters • easy-to-follow plots • popular topics
For children who are ready to read on their own.

Reading Paragraphs   Grades 2–3
• challenging vocabulary • short paragraphs • exciting stories
For newly independent readers who read simple sentences with confidence.

Ready for Chapters   Grades 2–4
• chapters • longer paragraphs • full-color art
For children who want to take the plunge into chapter books but still like colorful pictures.

STEP INTO READING® is designed to give every child a successful reading experience. The grade levels are only guides. Children can progress through the steps at their own speed, developing confidence in their reading, no matter what their grade.

Remember, a lifetime love of reading starts with a single step!

W9-DGV-601

created by

Visit us on the Web!
StepIntoReading.com
randomhouse.com/kids

Educators and librarians, for a variety of teaching tools, visit us at RHTeachersLibrarians.com

ISBN: 978-0-385-37499-6 (trade) — ISBN: 978-0-385-37500-9 (lib. bdg.)
Printed in the United States of America   10 9 8 7 6 5 4 3 2

nickelodeon

SpongeBob SQUAREPANTS

Moms
Are the Best!

By Sarah Wilson

Illustrated by Dave Aikins

Random House 🏠 New York

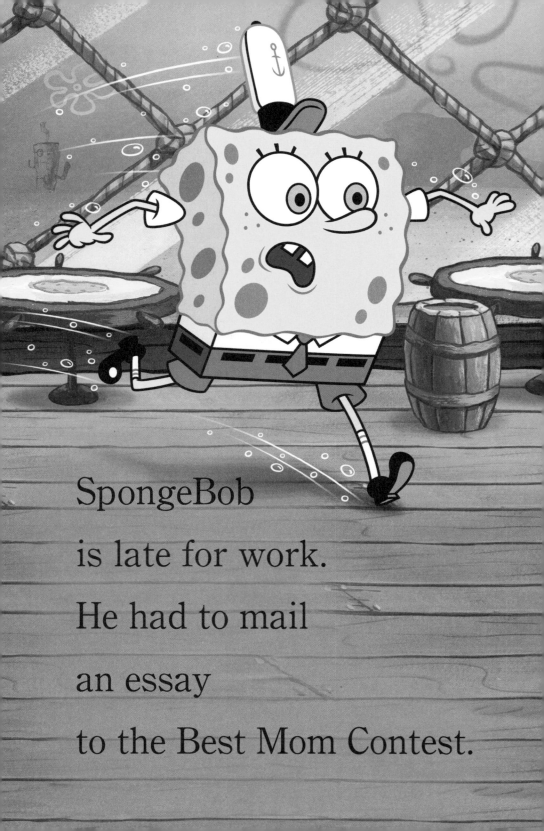

SpongeBob
is late for work.
He had to mail
an essay
to the Best Mom Contest.

Mr. Krabs gets
an idea.

"The Krusty Krab will have a special day for moms!" he says.

Mr. Krabs thinks
his plan will make him
lots of money!

Squidward calls
his mom.

SpongeBob calls
his mom.

It's the big day!

The Krusty Krab is full
of mothers and children.

Ring!

SpongeBob gets
a phone call.
It's his mother.

There is a leak
in her house.
She can't attend the lunch.

SpongeBob is sad.
Everybody's mom is there—
except his.

Squidward's mom
doesn't like
the Krusty Krab.

"Who can I complain to?"
she asks.

"Where is your mom?"
Mr. Krabs asks
SpongeBob.

SpongeBob quickly thinks
of an answer.

"My mom is a star,"
SpongeBob says.
"She has to go
someplace fancy
in her big car."

No one believes
SpongeBob.

The leak is fixed!
Now SpongeBob's mom
can go to the
Krusty Krab!

SpongeBob's essay
wins the contest!
His mother really is
a star—for a day!

SpongeBob's mom can do
anything she wants.
"I want to eat
at the Krusty Krab,"
she says.

She gets into

a big, fancy car.

At the Krusty Krab,
SpongeBob is sad.

"Too bad your mom
can't drive here
in her big car,"
Squidward says.

Suddenly,
a big car arrives.
SpongeBob's mom is
in it!

SpongeBob runs

to her.

Cameras flash.
People cheer.
Squidward can't believe
his eyes.

SpongeBob and
his mother
eat lunch.
"Moms are the best!"
he says.